Published by Stone Arch Books, an imprint of Capstone.
1710 Roe Crest Drive
North Mankato, Minnesota 56003
capstonepub.com

Library of Congress Cataloging-in-Publication Data

Names: Maddox, Jake, author. | Pryor, Shawn, author. | Maddox, Jake. Jake Maddox JV.
Title: Quarterback dreams / Jake Maddox ; [text by] Shawn Pryor.
Description: North Mankato, Minnesota : Stone Arch Books, 2022. | Series: Jake Maddox JV | Audience: Ages 9–12. | Audience: Grades 4–6. | Summary: Seventh-grader Darius Livingston is the star running back for his team, but what he really wants to do is play quarterback. Now that his team's season has been cancelled for lack of players, he may get a chance with the eighth-grade team, especially after both their quarterbacks are injured—but first he must remember that football is a team sport and stop trying to impress. Includes discussion questions, and writing prompts.
Identifiers: LCCN 2021012640 (print) | LCCN 2021012641 (ebook) | ISBN 9781663920256 (paperback) | ISBN 9781663910912 (hardcover) | ISBN 9781663910882 (ebook pdf)
Subjects: LCSH: Quarterbacks (Football)—Juvenile fiction. | Football stories. | Teamwork (Sports)—Juvenile fiction. | CYAC: Football—Fiction. | Teamwork (Sports)—Fiction. | LCGFT: Sports fiction.
Classification: LCC PZ7.M25643 Qtp 2021 (print) | LCC PZ7.M25643 (ebook) | DDC 813.6 [Fic]—dc23
LC record available at https://lccn.loc.gov/2021012640
LC ebook record available at https://lccn.loc.gov/2021012641

Editorial Credits
Editor: Alison Deering; Designer: Heidi Thompson; Media Researcher: Jo Miller; Production Specialist: Tori Abraham

Image Credits
Shutterstock: David Lee, back cover and throughout, Joe5APhotos, cover, Shawn Pecor, 1 and throughout

Design Elements: Shutterstock

QUARTERBACK
DREAMS

BY JAKE MADDOX

text by
Shawn Pryor

STONE ARCH BOOKS
a capstone imprint

TABLE OF CONTENTS

CHAPTER 1

GOTTA RUN, BUT I'D RATHER THROW!

Darius stood in the huddle with the rest of the seventh-grade football team. The Bulldogs were down nine points to the Castle County Rangers and on the fifty-yard line.

A few minutes later, Barrett returned with the next play. He was the team's starting wide receiver and one of Darius's best friends.

"So, what play are we running?" Corey, the Bulldogs quarterback, asked. He rubbed his hands together eagerly.

"I'm willing to bet I'm going to have to lead block again for Darius on a sweep," Marty, the starting fullback, joked.

Darius laughed. As the starting running back and focal point of the Bulldogs offense, he had little time to take a breather.

"I've already had sixteen carries. I'm good with just doing some pass blocking or being a decoy for a play or two," he said.

Barrett shook his head. "Sorry, Darius. Coach Ford called your number again. That's what happens when you're the fastest player on the team. Twenty-eight left sweep on three."

Just then the referee blew the whistle, marking the start of the fourth quarter.

Corey put his hand on Darius's shoulder. "You got this. All right, Bulldogs. Twenty-eight left sweep on three!"

The Bulldogs yelled "Break!" as they left the huddle and lined up against the Rangers defense.

Darius got into position a few yards behind his team's fullback. The quarterback held his hands under the center to receive the snap.

A Rangers linebacker pointed at Darius. "Their whole offense runs through number twenty-eight!" he hollered. "We stop him, and we win this!"

Corey yelled to get the play going. "SET! HUT-HUT-HUT!"

The Bulldogs center snapped the ball, and Corey took it. He began to turn toward his backfield. Marty ran past Corey and headed for the outside lane.

Getting the handoff from Corey, Darius followed Marty and the blockers, breaking free down the sideline. The crowd cheered as he ran over a linebacker and stiff-armed two Rangers defensive backs on his way to a long touchdown run.

The score was now 9–6. The Bulldogs were closing the gap.

The Bulldogs celebrated in the end zone, but Darius was exhausted. Barrett gave him a playful shove.

"You okay?" Barrett asked. "You do realize you just had a fifty-yard touchdown run, right? That was awesome!"

"I did make it look good, didn't I?" Darius joked. "But we've still got work to do, and there's plenty of time left in the game."

Even with Darius's run, the Bulldogs were still down by three. After the Rangers went three-and-out, the Bulldogs got the ball back at their own thirty-yard line.

As they huddled up again, Barrett came running from the sideline with the play they were supposed to run. "Halfback option pass on two," he said.

Corey nodded. "Smart play. Their defense has been stacking at least seven defenders at the line of scrimmage because we've given Darius the ball so many times. Even their defensive backs have been playing the run a lot this quarter. Barrett's going to be wide open. Darius will be able to throw an easy touchdown!"

Darius's eyes lit up. The thing he loved most about football was throwing. Last year, during the sixth-grade football season, he had his first opportunity to play quarterback and loved it. Playing QB put him in control of the offense, and he got to use his arm more than his feet.

But as a member of the seventh-grade team, Darius didn't get a chance to play QB—let alone throw the ball. The team had a small number of players on its roster, and not every player got the position he wanted. The coaches had seen Darius's speed and felt he would be best used as a running back.

In the huddle, Darius grinned. *The halfback option pass play will show the coaches how strong my arm is,* he thought excitedly. *Then maybe they'll let me take some snaps under center this season!*

"You better get ready for a deep ball, Barrett!" Darius said as the Bulldogs broke their huddle and got into position.

Corey received the snap from center and quickly pivoted to toss the ball to Darius. As Darius began to run, the Rangers defense shifted to stop him. As predicted, Barrett was wide open.

Darius stopped, looked downfield, and threw the ball. Barrett started running faster to catch up and made a beautiful one-handed grab. He coasted into the end zone, ball in hand.

The Bulldogs cheered as they scored the winning touchdown, bringing the final score to 12–9. Darius ran downfield and gave Barrett a leaping high five.

"Did you see that catch?" Barrett asked.

Darius grinned. "Of course! I've been waiting to throw the ball all season!"

As the team ran to the sidelines, Coach Ford gave Darius a high five. "Good game, Darius."

"What did you think of that pass, Coach?" Darius asked eagerly. "Did you see how far it went?"

Coach smiled. "You've got a strong arm, kid, and you came through when we needed it most. But you put a little too much power behind that throw. You're lucky Barrett made a great catch."

Darius flushed. He'd been expecting more compliments than that.

Coach looked sympathetic. "I know how much you want to play quarterback," he said, "but the team needs you at running back. Save the quarterback dreams for next season."

CHAPTER 2

CHANGES

When Darius arrived at practice the following Monday, he found Coach Ford in the locker room with his teammates. Everyone was standing around, still wearing their school clothes.

"Why isn't anyone getting dressed for practice?" Darius asked.

"Darius, come huddle up with the rest of the team," Coach Ford said. "Or should I say, what's left of it. I have some bad news. I found out today that Corey will be transferring to another school."

Darius's eyes lit up. *If Corey is moving to another school, maybe I'll get to make some throws as quarterback!*

"And Scott injured himself in a bike accident over the weekend," Coach continued. "He's out for the season. That means we no longer have a backup QB and starting kicker either . . . and we don't have enough players to field a team."

Grumbles and groans immediately filled the locker room. Darius didn't blame them. This was awful news. He'd known the team was small, but he hadn't realized they were at risk of not having enough players. Now he wouldn't get to play any position, let alone quarterback.

Darius raised his hand. "What if we all played a position on offense and defense? Could we finish the season?"

Coach Ford shook his head. "No. State rules won't allow us to do that," he explained to the team. "And we can't risk you boys overdoing it and exhausting yourselves."

"Great. I guess our season is over then," Barrett muttered. The rest of the players continued to grumble.

Coach Ford waved his hands, trying to settle down his team. "This doesn't mean the season is over for all of you. The league is allowing you to practice and play with the eighth-grade team for the rest of the season, and they can always use more depth."

"Do we have to try out again?" Marty asked.

Coach shook his head. "Nope. Just show up and be ready at the practice field with Coach Julian tomorrow at three p.m. I can't guarantee you'll see a ton of playing time, but it will at least get you prepared for eighth-grade football next season."

* * *

The next day, some of the seventh graders suited up for practice. Darius was feeling hopeful. He'd watched some of the eighth-grade team's games over the course of the season. Their offense struggled to move the ball.

"Okay, team, let's welcome our newest players!" Coach Julian shouted when everyone was gathered on the practice field.

"BULLDOGS WORK TOGETHER! BULLDOGS FOREVER!" the eighth graders yelled.

The coach continued. "I've seen you seventh graders play, and even though your team is small, your talent is big. We'll do what we can to get you on the field. The best players play, and they help their fellow teammates grow. That's how we win."

"All right, head to your position drills, and let's get started! Defense, go with Coach Carter! Special teams with Coach Davis! Running backs with Coach Taylor! Quarterbacks and receivers, come with me!"

The Bulldogs began to separate into their drill groups. Darius jogged over to Coach Julian.

"Coach?"

Coach Julian turned toward him. "Darius, right?"

Darius nodded. "Yes, sir."

"Shouldn't you be with the running backs?"

Darius took a deep breath. "Actually . . . I was wondering if I could join the quarterback drills. I'd like to take a shot at the position."

A pair of eighth graders, Eric and Stephen, overheard him as they made their way toward the drill station. One of the boys stopped and gave Darius an annoyed look.

"C'mon, Coach," Eric said, nodding to the player with him. "Stephen and I have QB all wrapped up. We don't need three players at the same position."

Stephen chimed in. "Yeah, and besides, there's no way we're letting a seventh grader take our spots."

"That sounds like a challenge," Darius replied.

Coach Julian stepped between the boys. "All right, that's enough. Darius, I've already got you penciled in at running back. We rely heavily on the running game, and you're going to get playing time there."

Disappointed, Darius started to turn away, but Coach Julian wasn't finished.

"But," the coach added, "show me what you got, and I'll think about it. Get ready to do some drills." He nodded at the two eighth graders. "Watch Eric and Stephen first, then you'll be up."

Eric went first. A group of wide receivers lined up to the right of him. The first receiver ran ten yards. When he began to slant to the left, Eric threw the ball. It landed right in the receiver's hands.

The next receiver ran a curl route. Again, Eric placed the ball right where it needed to go for an easy catch.

The third receiver ran fifteen yards upfield and made a sharp right turn for the sideline. Eric had the ball in the perfect spot as soon as the receiver opened his hands to make the catch.

Eric has a really good arm, Darius realized as he watched. *I need to be accurate if I'm going to compete with him. This might not be as easy as I thought.*

The final receiver ran a fly route running all the way toward the end zone for a deep pass. Eric heaved the ball downfield. The receiver slowed down a bit while waiting for the ball to get to him, but the catch was made.

"Nice job, Eric! Stephen, you're up! Let's go!" Coach Julian yelled.

Like Eric, Stephen was able to complete the drills successfully. But his passes lacked the speed that Eric's had.

Okay, Stephen doesn't have as strong an arm, but he can still make the necessary throws, Darius thought. *I've got to do a great job during my drills to have a shot at QB.*

"Darius, your turn! Show us what you've got," said the coach.

Darius grabbed a football and headed to his spot in the drill station. Eric and Stephen passed by him.

"Good luck, newbie," Eric said smugly.

Darius ignored him. *The only person I need to impress is the coach*, he reminded himself.

Darius's first throw was the slant pass. The wide receiver ran ten yards and began to slant to the left side of the field. Darius's pass sailed over the receiver's head, making the ball uncatchable.

Dang it, Darius thought, feeling frustrated. He knew Eric and Stephen were watching and judging.

Darius shook off his nerves for the curl route, throwing a perfectly timed ball to an eighth-grade receiver named Tyson. It hit the receiver's hands with a loud *THWACK!*

"Nice pass, Darius. That ball had some steam on it!" said Tyson, shaking his hands.

For his third and final throw, Darius threw to Barrett. He heaved a fifty-yard bomb that landed perfectly in his friend's hands.

"Nice catch, B!" Darius called.

"You got lucky on that last throw," Eric grumbled.

"And you still overthrew one target," said Stephen.

"Enough commentary, you two," said Coach Julian. He turned to Darius. "Not bad for your first go-round. I'm impressed, but Stephen and Eric are right. We have two QBs, so for now, I'm going to keep you as a running back."

Darius held back a sigh of frustration. He'd known it was a long shot, but he'd let himself feel hopeful.

Maybe next year, Darius told himself, taking his place with the rest of the running backs.

CHAPTER 3

YOUR NUMBER JUST GOT CALLED

Darius and his seventh-grade teammates
continued to practice with the eighth graders. Despite
Coach Ford's warning, Darius, Marty, and Barrett got
to play from time to time, filling in on certain plays to
give their older teammates a rest.

Darius was a third-string running back and
emergency QB. Marty played second-string fullback.
Barrett took the field as a second-string wide receiver.

Darius studied the playbook not only from the
running-back position, but also the quarterback

position. He watched what Eric and Stephen were doing during practice and took mental notes. No matter what, Darius was going to be ready.

The Bulldogs record stood at 3–3. They needed to win their next three games in order to make the playoffs. But their upcoming Friday night game against the Madison Monsters wasn't going to be easy. The Monsters were an aggressive team whose defense loved to blitz the quarterback—A LOT.

During their final practice before the game, the eighth-grade offense lined up to run a play against the first-team defense. Stephen was playing quarterback.

"All right, defense, see if you can stop the offense from making big plays!" Coach Julian yelled.

Stephen placed his hands under the center in order to receive the snap. He yelled to get the play going. "SET! HUT-HUT-HUT!"

The center snapped the ball to Stephen, who moved to take a three-step drop, preparing to throw the ball. But as he planted his back foot, there was a loud *POP!* Stephen shouted in pain as he fell to the ground.

Coach Julian ran out to Stephen. Darius and the rest of the team surrounded their teammate.

Stephen was trying to hold back the tears and pain, but it was too much to bear. "All I did was plant my foot. Just like I always do before throwing the ball," he gasped, clutching his ankle. "It hurts so much!"

"Call the medic!" Coach yelled. He turned back to Stephen. "Help is on the way, Stephen. We'll get you to a doctor and notify your parents."

* * *

The Bulldogs took the field against the Madison Monsters for their seventh game of the season on Friday evening. Eric was now leading the offense. Stephen had fractured his ankle and would be unable to play for the rest of the season.

Given the fact that Eric was the only remaining quarterback on the roster, Coach Julian had decided to promote Darius to second-string quarterback. There was no one else.

Darius was excited to serve as backup, but losing Stephen was a huge blow to the team. Even if Stephen hadn't been a great teammate, he was a great quarterback.

On the field, Eric grabbed the snap from the center. Darius had to admit, his teammate was doing a good job. The Bulldogs were up 17–9 late in the fourth quarter.

Eric took a three-step drop, eyeing a receiver downfield. But as he went to release the ball, one of the Monsters linebackers charged him. Eric's hand hit the opposing player's helmet—hard. The loud *CRACK!* could be heard across the field. The pass went incomplete.

Eric fell to the ground, clutching his hand in pain. "My hand! I can't move my fingers."

Coach Julian ran out on the field, followed by the team's trainer and medic. They brought Eric to the sideline. Darius was close enough to overhear what was going on.

"Looks like his hand is broken," said the medic.

"Broken? No! I want to play!" insisted Eric.

"I'm sorry, Eric," said Coach. "You can't play or throw the ball with a broken hand. They're going to take you to the hospital to get X-rays."

Darius was in disbelief. *A broken hand?* He'd wanted a shot at quarterback, but not like this. It was all so sudden.

Coach turned to Darius. "'I'm going to need you to run the offense for the rest of the game. There's only three minutes left. Are you up for it?"

Darius took a deep breath. He was glad he'd paid attention to the drills Stephen and Eric had run during practice. It was time to step up.

"I'm ready, Coach," he said. "Tell me what you need me to do."

Coach Julian nodded. "All you need to do is run the ball and stay in bounds to keep the clock running. We're up by eight, and they're out of time-outs. If we can get at least one first down on this drive, we're good."

"Okay, Coach," Darius replied. "Give me the plays."

"Start with halfback sweep left, then fullback sweep right, and QB option sneak," Coach Julian said.

"Got it!" said Darius.

He ran out on the field and got in the offensive huddle at the Bulldogs thirty-five-yard line. Barrett, Marty, and Tyson were already there.

"What's the play?" Tyson asked.

"Sweep left on two. No matter what, stay in bounds on every play. We've got to run out the clock," Darius said.

The Bulldogs yelled "BREAK!" before making their way to the line of scrimmage.

Darius was nervous, but he wasn't going to let the Monsters defense see it. As he put his hands under the center, he yelled, "READY! BULLDOG RED! SET! HUT-HUT!"

Darius took the snap and handed the ball off to Jordan, his running back. With Marty as lead blocker, Jordan managed a five-yard gain before being tackled.

The Bulldogs huddled back up. Darius called the next play. "Fullback sweep right on one. Break!"

Darius took the snap from center and tossed the ball to Marty. Running with the ball, Marty tried to make his way around the Monsters linebackers. He was only able to gain two yards, making it third down and three.

There were less than two minutes left on the clock. The Bulldogs went back to the huddle again.

Darius gave his team the next play. "QB option sneak on three. Ready, BREAK!"

Darius took the snap and faked a handoff to his running back. The Monsters defense was fooled.

They took off after the Bulldogs running back, thinking he had the ball.

Darius was clear to race up the field. He made his way past the fifty-, forty-, thirty-, twenty-, and finally the ten-yard line before he was tackled by a defensive back.

Darius looked up at the clock: one minute and five seconds left.

"Run victory formation! Victory formation!" Coach Julian yelled from the sideline.

Darius knew what that meant. He'd take the snap from center and take a knee for the next couple of plays, running down the clock. That would prevent the Monsters from getting the ball on offense and would secure victory for the Bulldogs.

The Bulldogs offense got back in the huddle, celebrating.

"Nice run, Darius!" Barrett said.

"Let's end this so we can hit the showers and get some pizza. I'm hungry!" Marty said.

Darius smiled. His first-ever drive as the Bulldogs quarterback had been a success. The Bulldogs record would soon move to 4–3, keeping their playoff hopes alive.

"You heard the coach, guys," Darius hollered. "Victory formation on one! BREAK!"

CHAPTER 4

TAKING THE REINS

On Saturday, Darius met up with Barrett and Marty. They were joined by another friend, Tisha, at the Grand Arcadium in town.

"So, how does it feel to be the Bulldogs starting quarterback?" Tisha asked as they finished a race-car game.

"I'm excited," Darius replied. He looked around, trying to figure out what to play next. "I can't wait for our next game so I can throw some deep bombs to Barrett!"

"And you know I'm going to look good when I catch them. When Coach lets me play, that is," Barrett joked.

"What did the coach say about Stephen and Eric?" Tisha asked.

Darius shook his head. "They're both out for the season. Coach told us after the game. Eric has a broken hand, and Stephen is going to be on crutches for a few months. It's like the unluckiest season of all time."

"Speaking of unlucky . . . it looks like we have company," Marty said.

"And they don't look happy," Barrett added, pointing across the arcade.

Darius looked toward the door and saw Eric, Stephen, and Tyson coming their way. It took Stephen a little longer due to him being on crutches. Eric was walking fine but sporting a cast on his right hand. Both boys had smirks on their faces as they approached.

"You got lucky out there last night, rookie," Eric said to Darius. "Next week's game is no joke. Angel Cove is going to eat you alive."

"Good thing Coach didn't need you throwing the ball," Stephen huffed, leaning on his crutches.

"Wow, you two sure are great teammates," Tisha muttered.

Darius was frustrated. "Look, I'm sorry you guys got hurt. I never wanted it to be this way. I just—"

"Oh, come on," Eric interrupted. "This is *exactly* what you wanted. You were gunning for our spots from day one. And now our seasons are over, and we can't help the team win."

"Yeah," Stephen agreed. "We have to win our last two games in order to make the playoffs, and there's no way that's happening with a seventh grader leading the offense."

"Hey, watch it!" Marty snapped at the injured quarterbacks. "It's not his fault the two of you got hurt."

"Seriously," Barrett added. "You should be grateful Darius was there to step in. If it weren't for him, we would have lost that game."

Tyson stepped between the two groups. "All right, enough. If Coach saw us arguing like this, we'd all be running laps right now." He looked at Eric and Stephen. "You two need to cool it. Yeah, it stinks that you're both hurt and out for the season, but we have to help each other if we want to win."

"Whatever," scoffed Eric. "If you want to hang out with these chumps, fine. Stephen and I are leaving. Later, losers."

Eric and Stephen walked away, leaving Tyson with Darius and the others.

"I'm sorry, y'all," Tyson said. "They're just upset."

"You mean they're just jerks," Barrett muttered.

Darius didn't disagree with his friend, but he didn't want to argue with Tyson. "Thanks for sticking up for me," he said. "We're going to hang here and play games awhile longer. Want to join us?"

"Sounds great," Tyson replied.

"And after, we're getting burgers and fries, right?" Marty asked. "My stomach is growling."

Tisha laughed. "Your stomach is *always* growling!"

"True, but he needs those calories to knock down linebackers!" Darius said with a laugh. "Let's go!"

* * *

On Monday, Darius suited up for his first practice as the Bulldogs starting quarterback. He couldn't wait to show his coach and teammates what he could do.

Leaving the locker room, the team headed out to the center of the practice field. Coach Julian was already there waiting. Eric and Stephen were standing next to him.

"As you know," Coach Julian began as the team huddled around, "we've lost both Eric and Stephen for the season. It's never fun to lose a teammate, but they'll be with us on the sidelines, rooting us on.

Darius will lead the offense during our final two games of the season. As you know, if we win both, we make the playoffs."

All the Bulldogs, except for Eric and Stephen, looked at Darius and nodded.

Darius smiled. "I won't let you guys down," he promised.

Coach Julian continued. "After last week's game, we're going to change up our offense a bit. Darius, you're going to lead a run-option offense. We're going to grind out yards, run down the clock, and keep the opposing team's offense off the field as much as we can. We won't be throwing much. Instead we'll use Darius's speed and our running backs to our advantage."

Darius couldn't believe what he was hearing. *Grind out yards? No throwing? We're just going to run the ball all the time?*

Darius opened his mouth to protest, but Coach held up a hand.

"With two big games coming up, this is our safest option," he said. "Darius is talented, but he's also new to the position. It isn't the time to take chances throwing the ball. We'll run our way to victory instead. Now, let's get practice started."

The Bulldogs huddled close. "Bulldogs on three. One, two, three . . . ," Coach said.

"BULLDOGS!"

CHAPTER 5

BREAKING THE RULES

That Friday, the Bulldogs were battling it out in a close game against the Angel Cove Blazers. The Bulldogs were trailing 13–10 in the fourth quarter. There were a little more than four minutes left on the clock.

Darius had spent almost the entire game handing the ball off to either his running back or fullback. He'd had only two passing plays—one that went incomplete, and the other a short toss to Tyson, one of his wide receivers.

Now, after a punt from the Blazers, Darius and the rest of the Bulldogs offense were about to take the field on their own twenty-yard line.

"Coach, the defense is expecting the run. Can we open up the offense a bit?" Darius asked.

Coach Julian thought about it for a second, then shook his head. "The running game's working," he said. "We can't risk turning the ball over with an interception. We can grind the ground game for eighty yards, score, and not give them enough time on offense."

"But Coach—," Darius started to say.

"Run a fullback middle, halfback sweep left, then QB option run right," Coach Julian said. "I'll send someone out to give you the next set of plays afterward."

Resigned, Darius headed out to the field to join the offensive unit in a huddle. Before Darius could announce the play, Barrett interrupted. "Let me guess, another running play?"

Darius nodded and sighed. "Yep. Coach thinks it's safer to run the ball and run down the clock. Fullback middle on one. BREAK!"

The offense got set at the line of scrimmage, and Darius took the snap from center. He handed it off to Marty, who made his way up the middle of the offensive line for a two-yard gain. But the next play, a halfback sweep left, resulted in a three-yard loss.

Darius was frustrated. *I'm tired of taking all these hits running quarterback sneaks and option plays,* he thought. *Why can't Coach believe in me enough to let me throw the ball more?*

The offense huddled up, facing a third and eleven. They needed eleven yards to get a first down.

"All right, Coach wants a QB option run right, but the defense is stacked at the line of scrimmage," Darius said. "They're waiting for us to run because that's all we've been doing today. I say we shake things up."

In the huddle, Tyson shook his head. "I don't think that's a good idea, Darius. We should run the plays Coach called."

Darius hesitated. He didn't want to disobey the coach, but more than anything he wanted to throw the ball. He knew he could do it.

"This is the right call," he said. "We're going to run a play-action fake, right on two. Barrett, Tyson, their defensive backs are going to let up on you after five yards because they're going to try to stop Jordan. Go long, and I'll throw it deep to one of you. BREAK!"

The offense got set at the line of scrimmage. Darius took the snap and faked a handoff to Jordan. Jordan, pretending he had the ball, continued up the right side of the field. The Blazers defense swarmed him.

With the ball tucked behind his back, Darius looked upfield. Both Barrett and Tyson were wide open!

Darius pulled back and threw the ball. Barrett sped up to make the catch, but the ball was just a little too high.

Oh, no, Darius realized. He'd overthrown it. Barrett wasn't going to be able to catch it.

But as Barrett strained for the ball that was beyond his reach, the Blazers defensive back tackled him. The pass was incomplete.

One of the referees threw a flag. "Pass interference, defense! Hitting a defenseless receiver as he was attempting to catch the ball. The ball will be placed at the spot of the penalty, the Blazers one-yard line. First down and goal, Bulldogs!"

Darius breathed a huge sigh of relief. He knew he'd gotten lucky. If not for the penalty, the Bulldogs would've been looking at a fourth down and eleven yards to go.

The Bulldogs offense huddled up near the end zone. Tyson ran to the sideline to get the play from Coach Julian. Darius was too nervous to look at the coach. He knew he was in trouble.

Tyson ran back to the huddle to give the offense the play. "Running back up the middle on one. And

Coach said if we don't run the play he called, we'll be in major trouble," said Tyson.

Darius exhaled. "You heard Tyson. Get us in the end zone, Jordan."

Darius and the offense got set at the line of scrimmage. Darius took the snap and handed the ball off to Jordan. He took it and leapt over the offensive line, crashing into defenders as he landed in the end zone—touchdown. The Bulldogs had taken the lead!

The Bulldogs celebrated on the field, high-fiving as they made their way to the sideline. The special teams unit prepared to kick the extra point.

Darius cautiously looked at Coach Julian. "Did you see that leap, Coach? Jordan went sky-high!" he exclaimed.

Coach Julian didn't respond. On the field, the extra point was good. The Bulldogs led 17–13 with less than two minutes left in the game.

Without a word to Darius or the offense, Coach Julian yelled, "Defense, get ready!"

Darius and the others went to the bench.

A moment later, Eric and Stephen walked over.

"You guys are in *big* trouble," Eric warned.

"You better hope the Blazers don't score, or Coach is going to be even more upset," Stephen said.

The Bulldogs defense held Angel Cove to four downs, turning the ball over to the Bulldogs with about one minute left in the game. Darius and the offense stood up to take the field, but Coach Julian had a different plan.

"Taylor! Take the second-team offense and run victory formation!" the coach ordered, staring at Darius and the first-team offense.

Darius began to sweat more than he had during the game. *Yep, I'm in big trouble.*

CHAPTER 6

BIG TROUBLE

After the game, the Bulldog locker room was very quiet. Darius sat silently, waiting for Coach Julian to speak.

"Listen up," Coach Julian said. "This win today put us a step closer to making the playoffs, but I'm disappointed in our offense." He looked around the room. "We are supposed to play as a team. That means *every* player respects his teammates—and me."

Darius looked down. He knew Coach Julian was talking about him.

Coach continued. "Sure, that pass got us a penalty that went in our favor, but we got lucky. If every player on this team did whatever he wanted, where would we be? Teams don't work that way. Are we in agreement?"

"Yes, Coach," the players said quietly.

"Without discipline, we'll lose our game next week. And then we can kiss the playoffs goodbye," he continued. "If a player or players break the rules, the whole team pays. During Monday's practice, we'll be learning some discipline—in the form of sprints."

The players grumbled. Coach didn't say Darius's name, but he didn't have to. Everyone knew who he was talking about.

"Thanks, Darius," one player griped.

"You just had to show off, and now we have to pay for it," another player muttered.

Darius kept his head down. The last thing that he'd wanted to do was anger his teammates and coaches.

I was just trying to prove that I can be a great quarterback, he thought. *And I blew it.*

* * *

As the players trickled out of the locker room, Darius sat next to his locker, still in his football uniform. Coach Julian was still there as well. Eventually, they were the only two left.

"Coach?" Darius said hesitantly. "I just . . . I wanted to say sorry. I'm sorry for not running the play you called. All I wanted to do was throw the ball. I wanted to prove I could move the team downfield—that way we don't have to run the ball so much." He looked at the floor. "Now the whole team is mad at me, and you're probably never going to let me play QB again."

Coach Julian sighed. "Darius, I know you enjoy throwing the football. And I know you're talented. You've got a strong arm. But it takes more than just a strong arm and throwing the ball as far as you can to be a quarterback. This is not just *your* team. The team is all of us: the players, coaches, and trainers."

"I understand now, Coach. I'm sorry," said Darius. "I hope the team can accept my apology too."

Coach put his hand on Darius's shoulder. "It takes guts and courage to admit when you've made a mistake. All you can do is tell them that you were wrong and why."

Darius sighed. "What if they don't accept my apology?"

Coach looked at Darius. "Well, I accept your apology. But the team will make their own decision, and you'll have to live with it. That's it." He paused. "Since we're talking about owning up to our mistakes, I should apologize to you too, Darius."

Darius was confused. "Apologize? Why? I'm the one who messed up."

"The moment I saw how fast you were, I made up my mind about having you run the ball," Coach said.

"I felt like it would work better for the team. And that might be true, but I also should have thought about you as an individual player. Helping you improve and play your best is important too. That's part of my job as a coach."

Darius smiled. "Thanks, Coach."

Coach paused. "If I'm being honest, I also worried a seventh grader might be too immature to lead an eighth-grade football team. But the team rallies around your energy and spirit."

"You think so?" Darius asked hopefully.

Coach nodded. "I do. But remember, we play for the good of the entire team, not just for ourselves."

"Got it, Coach," said Darius.

"Good. Hit the showers. I'll see you on Monday," said the coach.

CHAPTER 7

MAKING IT RIGHT

Darius spent the weekend thinking about what Coach Julian had said. He knew he needed to talk to his team. But that Monday, as he was about to enter the locker room, the two teammates he did *not* want to see—Eric and Stephen—walked up to him.

"Hey, newb," said Eric.

"Look, if you guys are going to harass me, I don't want to hear it," Darius snapped.

Stephen shook his head. He looked at Eric. "Actually . . . we wanted to apologize."

Darius was surprised. "Really? I thought you two hated me."

Eric shrugged. "We were just jealous that you were stepping on our turf. We didn't want to be shown up by a seventh grader."

"Coach Julian was pretty tough on you Friday. We've both been there. But like he said, we're a team. If we win this week, we're in the playoffs. We should support each other instead of trying to knock you down," Stephen said.

"But next time," Eric added, "run the plays Coach calls, okay?"

"Yeah, if there is a next time," said Darius.

"So, are we cool?" asked Stephen.

"We're cool," said Darius. He took a deep breath, exhaled, and entered the locker room.

Inside, some of his teammates gave him cold stares. Others didn't even look at him.

Darius walked to the center of the locker room, looked at his teammates and coaches, and cleared his throat. "Hey, guys, um . . . there's something I need to say to all of you."

He paused nervously. "I want to apologize for what I did on Friday night. I thought if I proved I could throw the ball and put points on the board, it would make things better for all of us. But I was playing for me, not the team."

A few of the players looked up and nodded.

"I can't take back what I did, but I'm sorry," Darius said. "It won't happen again."

The locker room was quiet. Kody, one of the starting linebackers, stepped toward Darius.

"Apology accepted," he said, putting a hand on Darius's shoulder. "We all make mistakes."

Another teammate, Adrian, spoke up. "What matters is that we learn from our mistakes, and it looks like you have. We're a team. No matter what happens, we've got your back."

The Bulldogs rallied around Darius in the center of the locker room. Darius felt relieved after getting that off his chest—and even better that the team was behind him.

I'm still a Bulldog, and that's the most important thing, he thought.

Darius shouted to his teammates: "WHO ARE WE?!"

"BULLDOGS!" the team replied.

Darius continued. "BULLDOGS WORK TOGETHER!"

"BULLDOGS FOREVER!"

Coach Julian stepped forward. "Okay, everybody, suit up and hit the practice field!" he said.

The Bulldogs put on their gear and got ready for practice. Coach Julian pulled Darius to the side.

"I'm proud of you," Coach Julian said.

"Thanks, Coach," Darius replied.

"Like I said the other day, you have a lot of potential, and it's my job to help you reach it," Coach continued. "There's someone I want you to meet."

CHAPTER 8

THROWING MECHANICS

After warming up with the rest of the team, the Bulldogs broke out into their player stations. Coach Julian took Darius and the wide receivers to their area. A younger woman was standing there waiting.

"Bulldogs, this is my daughter, Monica," said Coach Julian. "She played quarterback in a women's professional football league and interned as an offensive coach during college. Darius, Monica is going to help you with your throwing skills."

Coach Monica tossed a football to Darius. "Receivers, line up! Darius, show me what you've got. I'm going to yell a route for each receiver to run, and you make the throw, okay?"

"Got it!" replied Darius.

Tyson was the first receiver in the line.

"Ten-yard slant route. Go!" yelled Coach Monica.

Darius dropped back to pass as Tyson ran his route. Darius placed the ball a little high, but Tyson was able to make the catch.

Barrett was next in line.

"Fifteen-yard post left route. Go!" shouted Coach Monica.

Darius again dropped back and threw a strong pass. The ball was a little behind Barrett, but he was able to turn his body enough to make the catch.

Gabriel was next. "Fly route. Go!"

Darius dropped back and threw a forty-yard bomb. The ball sailed over Gabriel, but he picked up speed, stretched, and made a spectacular diving catch!

The other receivers were amazed. "Wow, what a catch! Way to go, Gabriel!" said Barrett.

Darius looked to Coach Monica, waiting for her feedback. "You've got a lot of arm strength. But you're throwing the ball *at* your receivers instead of *to* them. Arm strength means nothing if you can't consistently place the ball where the receiver can catch it. Control of the ball is important. You're throwing with your arm rather than your whole body. We're also going to have to work on your foot placement."

"Whole body? Foot placement? What do you mean?" asked Darius.

"Using your whole body to throw the ball takes the stress off your arm," Coach Monica explained. "And proper foot placement will help with accuracy. Right now you're just throwing as hard as you can and betting on your receivers to make the catch. Better throwing mechanics will make you a better QB."

Coach Monica grabbed a football for herself and tossed another over to Darius. "Let's work on your footwork first. Stand to the left of me and mimic my movement for a three-step drop. Okay?"

Darius nodded. Coach Monica moved slowly as she took three steps back. Darius copied her movement.

"Taking a three-step drop will help you with your timing," Coach Monica explained. "It also forces you to plant your back foot before making the throw."

Darius tried the move again, this time with Coach Monica watching.

"Good," she said. "Now we're going to do that again, but this time we'll add a throw. You want to plant your right foot and throw with your whole body. That means that you'll be using your throwing arm and turning your waist as you release the ball. That should help you be more accurate when throwing to a receiver. Watch me first."

Coach Monica turned to the group of receivers. "Barrett, run a fly route. Go!"

Barrett ran downfield as Coach Monica performed a three-step drop. She stopped, stepped forward, and planted her right foot. Then she wound up and threw a crisp, deep spiral down the field. It landed perfectly in Barrett's hands, thirty yards away.

The whole time, Darius studied Coach Monica's movements and throwing form. Her advice was starting to click.

"Nice catch, Barrett!" Coach Monica called.

"Thanks, Coach! You made that look easy!" Barrett replied. He jogged closer and gave Coach Monica a high five.

Darius was eager for his turn. "Can I try now?"

"Go for it," said Coach Monica. "Tyson, run a fly route. Go!"

Tyson blazed down the sideline. Darius took his three-step drop, stopped, stepped forward, and planted his left foot. He performed the same throwing motion Coach Monica had. The ball flew so far down the field that Tyson couldn't catch up with it.

Darius shook his head in frustration. "I missed Tyson completely. What did I do wrong?"

"Well, you did everything that you were supposed to do, but you still need to ease up on your arm strength," Coach Monica said. "It'll take some work to balance it out."

"It didn't even feel like I threw it that hard," said Darius.

"That's what happens when you throw with your whole body and not just with your arm," Coach Monica told him. "And the more we practice, the more touch you're going to be able to put on the ball. You'll be able to put the ball where the receivers can catch it."

"Can we keep working on this?" Darius asked.

"We're going to work on it all week," she replied. "We'll get you ready!"

CHAPTER 9

FINDING THE TARGET

As the week went along, Darius continued to work with Monica during practice. Thanks to her advice and coaching, his quarterback skills were improving.

"All right, Darius, let's see if all of our hard work this week has been paying off," Coach Monica said at practice midweek. "Receivers, line up!"

Tyson was first in line.

"Fifteen-yard curl route, go!" Coach Monica yelled.

Darius began to drop back, repeating to himself, *Three-step drop, plant your right foot, step forward, and use your body to make the throw.*

He did all the steps and threw a beautiful pass. The ball went right where it was supposed to. Tyson easily caught it at the end of his route.

Yes! Darius cheered silently.

Gabriel was next.

"Ten-yard post, go!" Monica yelled.

Again, Darius dropped back. He repeated the steps in his head while making his throw, a crisp, accurate pass. Gabriel made a clean sideline catch, keeping his feet inbounds.

Two for two!

Barrett was next.

"Go deep, Barrett!" Coach Monica yelled.

Barrett took off, moving like a bullet train downfield.

Darius took a deep breath. *This pass is going to be a long one. I better not overdo it. I've got this.*

He dropped back and threw a perfect, deep ball that landed right in Barrett's hands!

"Three for three!" Darius yelled. He and Coach Monica high-fived.

"Wow, if you throw deep passes like that during the game, there's nobody that can stop us!" Barrett exclaimed.

"Your passes had plenty of speed and power, but this time, they didn't hurt my hands!" Tyson said. "Great touch!"

Coach Julian interrupted. "Monica, do you think the offense is ready to scrimmage against the defense?"

Darius looked at Coach Monica. "We're ready. Let's do this!"

* * *

The Bulldogs scrimmaged for the rest of practice. Darius tried his best to concentrate on his footwork and throwing motion, but putting it all together under pressure was a challenge. He'd overthrown or underthrown his targets several times.

With the ball at the fifty-yard line, Darius joined the huddle to call the play. "Play action fake, on two. Tyson, Barrett, do your best to get open. BREAK!"

The offense approached the line of scrimmage as Darius got under center.

"READY!" Darius yelled. "BULLDOG RED! SET! HUT-HUT!"

Darius grabbed the snap and faked the handoff to Jordan. Most of the defense took the bait and began to follow him, leaving Barrett and Tyson open. They ran downfield, signaling for the ball.

Darius ran through Coach Monica's advice as he prepared to throw the ball. *Okay, plant your left foot, use your body, make the throw. Plant your left foot, use your body, make the—*

From out of nowhere, a linebacker pummeled Darius, knocking the ball out of his hands. Another defender grabbed the ball and ran it down the field for a touchdown.

Barrett helped Darius up off the ground. "You okay, man?" he asked.

Darius nodded his head. "Yeah, I'm okay. You and Tyson were wide open, and I held onto the ball too long."

The Bulldogs offense ran toward the sideline. The coaches were there waiting.

"Shake it off, offense!" Coach Monica said. "If we don't move the ball against Middletown on Friday, we don't have a chance."

"Sorry about the fumble," Darius said.

Coach Monica looked over at Darius. "You're overthinking your throw," she said. "I can see it as you play."

"I just want to get it right. I don't want to let the offense down," said Darius.

"I understand, and I'm glad you're taking my advice to heart, but it's not about being perfect," she replied. "Don't think about the steps you have to take. You know how to throw the ball now. I've seen it. Let your body and your brain work together. Don't overthink it. Just play."

Darius nodded. "Okay, I'll do my best."

"Let's start the next drive with a mix of quick slant passes and some runs up the middle," Coach Monica suggested to the offense. "The quick slant pass will get Darius to release the ball fast, and Barrett and Tyson can outrun the defense for some good gains."

Darius nodded, and the offense took the field at their thirty-yard line. The Bulldogs defense was ready for them.

Darius took the snap and quickly tossed the ball to Tyson, who grabbed the pass and ran upfield for a thirty-five-yard gain. First down!

On the next play, Darius ran a slant right pass, attempting to throw the ball to Barrett. But the defense was ready. The defensive back covering Barrett swatted the pass away before Barrett could catch it.

"You're staring down your receiver, Darius!" Coach Monica yelled. "During a pass play, it's okay to look over all your receivers. That way the defense doesn't automatically know where you're throwing."

"Got it, Coach!" Darius yelled. *Note to self: Don't stare down your receiver.*

Finally, it was fourth down and one. Darius and the offense ran back to the sideline.

"What are we going to do, Coach?" Darius asked.

"They're going to expect us to run a QB sneak or a running-back dive play to get a yard," Coach Monica replied. "The defense will be focused on Jordan. Let's run a running-back dive fake. The defense will think it's a running play and try to tackle Jordan. Tyson will be wide open in the end zone. You can throw to him for a touchdown."

Darius nodded a bit nervously. Putting together everything Coach Monica had taught him was a lot, and he hadn't connected on a lot of passes during the scrimmage. His confidence was a bit shaky.

But the rest of the offense didn't seem worried. Jordan slapped Darius's shoulder pads. "We've got this! Let's do it!" he said.

The offense ran back on the field. Darius took the snap and faked the handoff to Jordan. The running back leapt in the air as if he had the ball. As predicted, the defenders swarmed him.

Darius looked over to see Tyson wide open near the end zone. He threw a long pass straight to Tyson's hands for the touchdown!

Darius pumped his fist proudly! *I can do this,* he thought. *We're going to win this Friday and be playoff-bound!*

CHAPTER 10

WIN AND YOU'RE IN!

It was the final game of the regular season for the Bulldogs. They were up against the Middletown Mayhem. The team was known for being ferocious on defense. They led the conference in quarterback sacks and interceptions.

Darius was stretching as Eric and Stephen walked up to him. Stephen was now on one crutch instead of two, but he was still far away from being able to play football. Eric's throwing hand was still in a cast.

"Good luck, Darius," said Eric.

"Be on the lookout for their defensive backs. They're really good at swatting passes and guarding wide receivers," Stephen warned.

"Thanks, guys," Darius replied.

Eric and Stephen walked away as Darius continued stretching. He needed to focus on the game at hand. The Bulldogs spot in the playoffs depended on it.

* * *

Finally it was game time. The Bulldogs offense took the field on their own twenty-five-yard line. Darius was in the huddle, ready to call the play.

"Fullback middle blast on two, BREAK!" said Darius.

The offense broke the huddle and set up at the line of scrimmage. Darius received the snap and handed the ball off to Marty, who barreled through the middle of the line for a twelve-yard gain!

"First down!" the referee signaled.

The next play was a receiver left post route, with Tyson cutting across the middle of the field. Darius had his eyes locked on Tyson the whole play and threw a bullet pass toward the receiver.

From out of nowhere, a Mayhem defensive back intercepted the pass.

The Bulldogs tried to tackle their opponent but fell short. The Mayhem defender ran forty-five yards for a touchdown. After the extra point, the Bulldogs trailed 7–0.

Darius gritted his teeth in frustration. He couldn't believe he'd turned the ball over. He'd done exactly what Coach Monica had told him *not* to do: stared down his receiver.

"Shake it off, Darius," Coach Monica said as the offense jogged back to the sideline. "It's okay. There will be more chances for us to score."

In the second quarter, the Bulldogs offense was able to catch up with a long touchdown run from

Jordan, which tied the game 7–7. After a three-and-out from the Mayhem offense, the Bulldogs received the punt at their thirty-eight-yard line.

Coach Julian gave Darius the play as the offense was about to take the field again. "Receiver right slant deep. Good luck."

Darius ran to the huddle, gave the play, and the offense set up at the line of scrimmage. Following the snap, Darius took a three-step drop and locked his eyes on Barrett. Avoiding a blitzing linebacker and pushing off a defensive lineman, he threw a deep pass—intercepted!

As the other Bulldogs went to chase down the defender with the ball, Darius was blasted by another Mayhem player. The vicious block stopped him cold. Darius looked up from the ground just in time to see the Mayhem score another touchdown off an interception.

"Keep giving us these easy points!" one of the Mayhem players yelled.

Another Mayhem player hollered, "That hit took a lot out of him. He's scared of us now!"

Tyson and Barrett jogged over and helped Darius off the ground.

"Are you okay?" Tyson asked.

"That dude hit you pretty hard," Barrett added.

"I-I'm okay," Darius replied. "I'll be fine."

The Bulldogs offense left the field just before the Mayhem kicked the extra point. They now led the Bulldogs 14–7.

The coaches met Darius on the sideline.

"That hit looked really rough," said Coach Julian. "Do you need the trainer to check on you?"

"No, Coach, he just shook me up a bit. I'm okay, but . . . I don't think I should throw the ball for a while," Darius forced himself to say. "I'm costing us the game with my turnovers."

"It's almost halftime," Coach Monica said. "You and I are going to have a talk."

CHAPTER 11

BACK IN THE GAME

"Listen," Coach Monica told Darius in the locker room at halftime. "We're only behind by a touchdown, and we've got two quarters to go. We can get back in the game."

"Not if I keep throwing interceptions," Darius said.

"The only reason they intercepted you twice is because you're staring down your receivers. When you're dropping back to pass, you can't stare down your target. Defenses read that and can take advantage of you," Coach Monica said.

"I keep telling myself that, but in the middle of the play, I forget," Darius said. "We have to find a different way to move the ball."

"I've got an idea," said Coach Monica. "Coach Julian, can you come here?"

Coach Julian walked over to them.

"I think we should start the next offensive series with short passes to our running backs," Coach Monica suggested. "Jordan and Marty can come around from the backfield to open up the passing game, and give Darius some confidence throwing the ball."

"Yeah, that could work!" Darius smiled.

Coach Julian nodded. "Let's give it a try. Outside of Jordan's touchdown run, their defense has been stopping our running plays with little or no gain."

"My head is back in the game. I'm ready!" said Darius.

* * *

At the beginning of the third quarter, the Mayhem started on offense. After a long, slow drive that ate up most of the third-quarter clock, the Mayhem turned the ball over at the Bulldogs twenty-yard line due to a missed field goal. Darius and the offense finally took the field with two minutes left.

"Give us another easy turnover!" one of the Mayhem players yelled at Darius.

Darius ignored him. He grabbed the snap, took a three-step drop, and tossed a crisp pass to the right side of the field. Marty turned out of the backfield for a nineteen-yard gain and first down!

On the next play, Darius threw a pass out of the backfield to Jordan for another big gain. They were now at the Mayhem forty-yard line.

The Mayhem attempted a quarterback blitz on the next play. Darius managed to avoid it and threw a sideline pass to Tyson in the end zone. Touchdown!

The Bulldogs celebrated as the special teams unit went to kick the extra point to tie the game.

"Nice catch, Tyson!" said Darius, high-fiving his teammate.

"Thanks," Tyson said. "You threaded the needle on that pass!"

But on the field, the Bulldogs kicker missed the extra point. They trailed the Mayhem, 14–13, as the third quarter came to a close.

* * *

The final quarter was a constant back and forth. Neither team was able to make much headway.

Finally, late in the fourth quarter, the Mayhem kicked a field goal, extending their lead to four points. With a little under two minutes left, the score was 17–13.

Darius and the offense waited to take the field as the Mayhem prepared to kick off to the Bulldogs. Suddenly, the Mayhem changed their kickoff formation!

"ONSIDE KICK! ONSIDE KICK!" Coach Julian yelled.

The Mayhem were going to try an onside kick in an attempt to gain control of the ball again. It would keep the Bulldogs offense on the sideline.

The Mayhem kicker punted the ball ten yards as his teammates on the field attempted to recover it. Luckily the Bulldogs snagged the ball at their forty-yard line. A minute and thirty-two seconds remained on the clock, with no time-outs left.

The Bulldogs offense took the field. Darius called the play, and the offense went to the line of scrimmage. Taking the snap, Darius threw a quick slant pass to Barrett for a ten-yard gain and a first down.

Darius and his teammates hurried upfield. They got to the line of scrimmage to run the next play as the clock ticked down to one minute.

Taking the snap, Darius threw a halfback pass to Jordan. He avoided the Mayhem defenders and sprinted for twenty yards before running out of bounds, stopping the clock with forty-five seconds remaining.

On the Mayhem thirty-yard line, Darius took the snap. He stepped up in the pocket and threw a laser to Tyson near the left sideline. Tyson made the catch, putting the Bulldogs at the Mayhem fifteen-yard line with thirty seconds left!

Darius and the rest of the offense were exhausted, but they were so close to the end zone. They could do this!

In the huddle, Darius gave the play. "End zone receiver fade on one, BREAK!"

The offense lined up, and Darius took the snap. Before he could even take two steps back, he was sacked by three Mayhem defenders for a five-yard loss.

Darius pushed the defenders off him and scrambled to his feet. "We have to stop the clock!" he yelled to his teammates. "Go, go, go!"

The offense hurried to line up. Darius took the snap and downed the ball at the Mayhem twenty-yard line, stopping the clock with five seconds left.

Barrett ran to the sideline to get the final play of the game.

If we score a touchdown, we win, Darius thought. *We have to get there!*

A moment later, Barrett returned. "Receiver option post," he said.

The offense broke the huddle and got ready for their final play. Everything seemed to move in slow motion as Darius got ready to take the snap from center. He could feel his heart beating rapidly.

"READY! BULLDOG RED! SET! HUT-HUT-HUT!" Darius hollered.

Taking the snap, Darius stepped back, ready to throw the ball. Barrett cut across the goal line. He was wide open!

But just as Darius was about to throw the ball, one of the Mayhem linebackers tried to sack him.

Darius quickly moved to avoid one defender, then another. He began running toward the end zone. Marty trailed behind him.

Darius was getting closer and closer to the end zone. He was going to score!

Suddenly, one of the Mayhem defensive backs was at the two-yard line. He looked more than ready to tackle Darius.

Darius acted on instinct. He pitched the ball behind to Marty, who caught it and raced into the end zone for the touchdown.

The Bulldogs had won! They were going to the playoffs!

Darius and his teammates cheered in the end zone as the rest of the Bulldogs ran over to celebrate.

"How did you know I was going to catch your pitch?" Marty asked.

"I didn't!" Darius answered. "I remembered what Coach Monica told me. I just need to let go and play, and it worked!"

Tyson, Marty, and Barrett put Darius on their shoulders.

Darius cheered, "BULLDOGS WORK TOGETHER!"

"BULLDOGS FOREVER!" the team replied.

GLOSSARY

advantage (ad-VAN-tij)—something that benefits or helps

balance (BAL-uhns)—to keep even or equal

blitz (BLITS)—a play in which several defending players charge toward the quarterback to tackle him or her

commentary (KOM-uhn-ter-ee)—spoken or written discussion in which people express opinions about someone or something

decoy (DEE-koi)—a person or thing that attracts people's attention so they will not notice someone or something else

defense (di-FENS)—the team that does not have possession of the ball. This side tries to keep the offensive side from getting the ball into their end zone.

down (DOWN)—a play in which the offense tries to advance the ball down the field; today teams get four downs to go 10 yards

formation (for-MAY-shuhn)—the position of football players before a snap

fracture (FRAK-chur)—a broken or cracked bone

fumble (FUHM-buhl)—when a football player drops the ball or it is knocked out of his or her hands by another player

huddle (HUD-uhl)—a gathering of football players on a team before a play

interception (in-ter-SEP-shun)—a pass caught by a defensive player

mechanics (muh–KAN–iks)—the details about how something works or is done

offense (aw-FENSS)—the team that is in control of the ball and is trying to score

punt (PUNT)—a play where the ball is dropped from the hands and kicked before it touches the ground

roster (ROSS-tur)—a list of players on a team

sack (SAK)—when a defensive player tackles the opposing quarterback behind the line of scrimmage

scrimmage (SKRIM-ij)—a practice game

tackle (TACK-uhl)—to stop another player by knocking him or her to the ground

DISCUSSION QUESTIONS

1. Why do you think Darius wanted to play quarterback instead of running back? Do you think he was better at one position or the other? Talk about your opinion.

2. Darius takes matters into his own hands when he ignores Coach's play and runs his own. Have you ever played a team sport where someone didn't do what the coach said? Talk about what happened when the coach's instructions weren't followed.

3. Darius was worried about throwing the ball during the first half of the final game. Why do you think that was? Have you ever been in a situation where you felt nervous about something you were normally good at? Talk about how you dealt with it.

WRITING PROMPTS

1. At the end of the final game, Darius makes the toss to Marty to help the Bulldogs win. Have you ever experienced a winning moment like that, either with a team or on your own? Write a paragraph about your experience and how it made you feel.

2. This story is told from Darius's point of view, but there are times where it's useful to consider a story from another character's perspective. Try rewriting Chapter 2 from either Eric or Stephen's point of view.

3. Coach Monica tells Darius he needs to work on his throwing mechanics in order to be a better quarterback. Write a list of things she suggested Darius work on and explain why each was important.

MORE ABOUT FOOTBALL

Football is the most popular spectator sport in the United States. In a 2018 poll, 37 percent of adults named it as their favorite sport. And in 2019, the National Football League (NFL) made more than $15 billion from its 32 teams. Want to know more about the sport? Here are some interesting facts you may not know.

Walter Camp is known as the "Father of American Football." He helped create football's line of scrimmage as well as the system of downs used by the offense when they take the field.

The first American football game took place on November 6, 1869. The game was played in New Brunswick, New Jersey, between Rutgers and New Jersey (now known as Princeton University).

The first televised football game was in 1939. It aired on only 500 TV sets in the United States.

The "huddle" was created by quarterback Paul Hubbard in the 1890s. Hubbard was deaf and worried other teams might understand the hand gestures and signals he showed to his teammates. To avoid that, he decided to bring his teammates together in a circle in order to call plays.

Football helmets weren't mandatory for players until 1939!

The NFL was founded in 1920. Since then, only the Miami Dolphins have played a perfect season (17–0–0). In 1972, they won all fourteen regular season games and three postseason games, including Super Bowl VII.

An American football field is 120 yards long and 53.3 yards wide.

College and professional football games are 60 minutes long, broken down into four 15-minute quarters. High school games are typically 48 minutes long.

LOOKING FOR MORE
FOOTBALL ACTION?
THEN PICK UP . . .

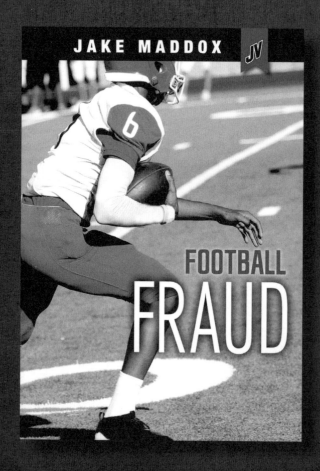

JAKE MADDOX

JV

FOOTBALL
FRAUD

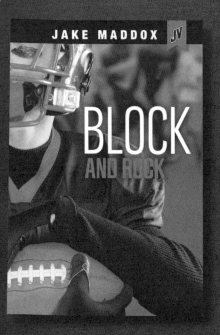

JAKE MADDOX JV

BLOCK
AND ROCK

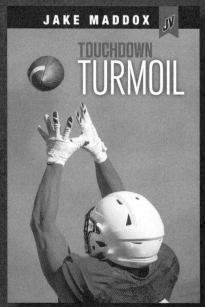

JAKE MADDOX JV

TOUCHDOWN
TURMOIL

capstonepub.com

ABOUT the AUTHOR

Shawn Pryor is the creator and co-author of the graphic novel mystery series Cash and Carrie, co-creator and author of the 2019 GLYPH-nominated football/drama series Force, and author of *Kentucky Kaiju*. He has also written several books for Capstone, including *Nat Turner's Rebellion*, as well as books in series such as Jake Maddox Sports Stories, Jake Maddox Adventure, and Kids' Sports Stories. Shawn once was a legendary backyard quarterback but retired from backyard football to pursue a career in writing.

photo by Alison Heck